Whisker Haven
T A L E S
with the
palace pets

The Cake-tillion

By Thaddeus Dilday
Illustrated by the Disney Storybook Art Team

A Random House PICTUREBACK® Book
Random House 🏠 New York

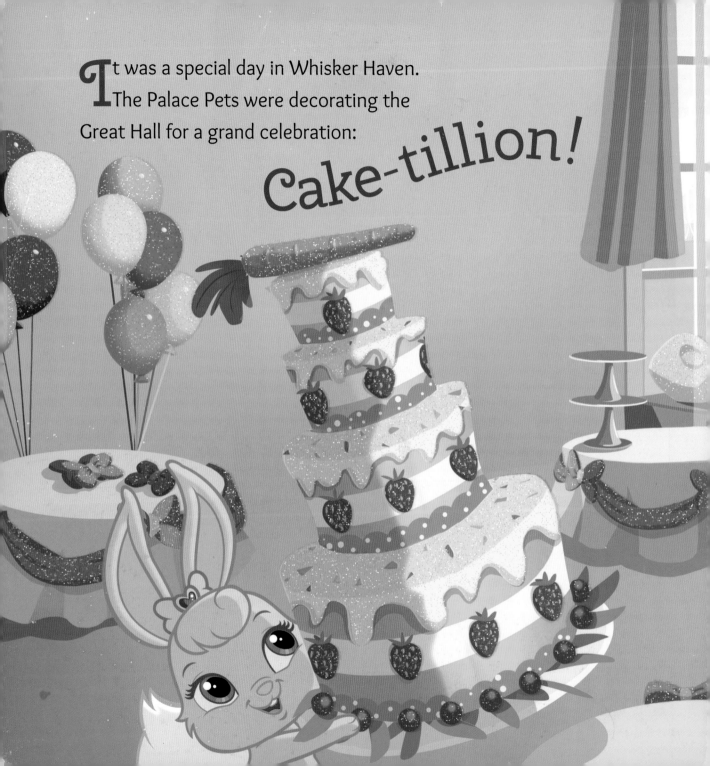

It was a special day in Whisker Haven. The Palace Pets were decorating the Great Hall for a grand celebration:

Cake-tillion!

Suddenly, Sultan raced in.
He whipped past Berry and sent
Treasure spinning—SPLAT!—
right into the cake!

"Sorry," said Sultan, licking icing off Berry's head.

Berry giggled, then turned serious. "How are we going to have Cake-tillion without cake?" she asked.

"Don't worry," said Treasure. "Lily will come through that door any second with whisker cakes!"

The pets turned to the door. They
waited . . . and waited . . . and waited.
But Lily never came.

The pets were worried.

"Let's go look for her," Sultan said.

Sultan, Berry, and Treasure raced across the Pawlace and found Ms. Featherbon perched on the edge of her birdbath.

"We need help finding Lily!" Berry cried.

Ms. Featherbon tossed glitterbits into her birdbath.

"Paw-doodily-dee, paw-doodily-dined!" she sang. "Show us Lily, whom we want to find!"

An image of Lily appeared in the birdbath. She was lost in the woods!

"We have to rescue Lily!" exclaimed Treasure.

Sultan raced away. Treasure, Berry, and Ms. Featherbon followed close behind.

Soon the friends reached the forest. Lily was nowhere in sight. Just then, Berry heard a noise.

With her ears guiding her,
Berry led her friends over rocks
and around trees, until . . .

they found Lily!

Lily was happy to see her friends!

"We're glad you're okay," said Berry. "Now let's get these cakes to Whisker Haven!"